THE HUNCHBACK
OF NOTRE DAME

THE HUNCHBACK OF NOTRE DAME

By Victor Hugo

Adapted by Diana Stewart
Illustrated by Charles Shaw

RSVP
RAINTREE
STECK-VAUGHN
PUBLISHERS
The Steck-Vaughn Company

Austin, Texas

Library of Congress Number: 81-5151

Library of Congress Cataloging-in-Publication Data

Stewart, Diana.
  The hunchback of Notre Dame.

  (Raintree short classics)
  SUMMARY: Retells in simple language the tale of the hunchbacked bellringer of medieval Notre Dame, Quasimodo, whose love for the gypsy dancer, Esmeralda, had tragic consequences.
  1. France—History—Medieval period, 987–1515—Juvenile fiction. [France—History—Medieval period, 987–1515—Fiction 2. Paris (France)—Fiction] I. Hugo, Victor, 1802–1885. Notre Dame de Paris. English. II. Shaw, Charles, 1941– III. Title. IV. Series.
PZ7.S84878Hu   [Fic.]   81-5151

ISBN 0-8172-1671-5 hardcover library binding

ISBN 0-8114-6827-5 softcover binding

14 15 16 17 18 19   99 98 97 96 95 94 93 92

CONTENTS

I

THE PRIEST TAKES A FOUNDLING

The cathedral of Notre Dame in Paris is an awesome building. From its high towers, one has a bird's-eye view of the sprawling city and the river Seine below. For hundreds of years the church has stood strong against wars and revolutions. It has seen many strange and wonderful sights. Our story here, however, is perhaps one of the strangest stories in its history.

In 1467 — fifteen years before our tale begins — a foundling, an orphan boy, was left on a wooden bench beside the great front doors of Notre Dame. The custom of the time was to leave orphans there in the hope that some kind person would adopt the child.

One day two women entering the church looked at the wooden bench and saw a little crying, twisting creature.

"What in the world is that, sister?" one exclaimed.

" 'Tis not a child," the other said. " 'Tis an ape — a monster!"

The shapeless, moving mass was indeed a terrible sight. It was not a baby but a child of four years of age. Its head was so deformed it was hideous. It had no neck at all. One eye — the other was blind — was filled with tears.

"No one will adopt such a child!" the women exclaimed.

But they were wrong. A young priest — Claude Frollo — had been listening to the women. He was a serious young man with a high forehead and piercing black eyes. He had recently lost his family in the plague — the black death — that swept France. Now he stepped forward and looked down at the screaming child. Pity filled his heart.

"I adopt this child," said the priest, and he stooped and picked up the poor, deformed wretch.

Fifteen years passed quietly after the poor misshapen boy came to live at the Church of Notre Dame. During that time Dom Claude Frollo became an Archdeacon — the chief priest of Notre Dame. His face grew even more sober. He lost all of his hair except for a fringe over his ears. Quasimodo — for that is the name he gave the child — grew into a man of twenty. Not many citizens of Paris, however, would have called Quasimodo a man.

If he was ugly as a child, he was even uglier now. His head was covered with red hair. His teeth had grown sharp and crooked and jagged. His nose was large and misshapen. His blind eye was covered with skin and looked like an enormous boil. Between his shoulders was a huge hump, and his legs were so strangely put together they touched only at the knees. In all, he looked like a giant who had been broken into pieces and put together at random.

At the age of fourteen, Dom Claude made Quasimodo bell-ringer of Notre Dame, and a new curse came upon the poor wretch. The bells were so loud that they broke his eardrums, and he became deaf. Being deaf, he spoke very little, and when he did speak, his voice was deep and gruff.

When people saw him on the streets now, the women screamed and covered their faces in horror. The men jeered and mocked him: "Look! There is Quasimodo the bell-ringer! It is Quasimodo the hunchback of Notre Dame! Quasimodo the one-eye! Oh, hideous ape! And as mean as he is ugly! 'Tis the devil himself!"

The outside world was so unkind that Quasimodo seldom left the great church. It was his home and his joy. He loved every niche and corner. He loved every statue and stone. And he loved his bells. He caressed them, talked to

7

them, understood them — from the chimes in the steeple to the great bells in the tower. And it was true that theirs were the only voices that he could still hear.

As he pulled the ropes on the giant bells, his hands and arms became very strong. Often he could be seen crawling up the outside of the huge towers like a giant lizard — and people hated and feared him even more.

Men might call him a devil, but to do him justice, he had not always been like that. He might have been a kind and loving child, but wherever he went he was despised, rejected, mocked, and laughed at. As he grew older, he learned to hate everything around him — everything, that is, but the great church, his wonderful bells, and his master Dom Claude.

Quasimodo followed his master around like a faithful puppy, wanting only to please. The priest had first taught him to talk, and later — after Quasimodo became deaf — Dom Claude had developed a sign language. The poor wretch would have done anything for his master.

On the night of January 6, 1482, when our story begins, Dom Claude made a very strange request of Quasimodo: "I want you to bring me the gypsy girl Esmeralda!" he said.

So the two men went out of the church together. The night was dark and few people were on the streets. They had not gone far before they spotted the gypsy on her way home. She was a beautiful young creature of sixteen, with black, flowing hair and a graceful figure. She was a dancer and made her living performing on the streets in the hopes that people would throw her coins. With her was the only thing she loved — a small, dainty white goat.

As Esmeralda turned a corner, Quasimodo leaped upon her. He grabbed her by the arms and would have carried her away, but the poor, frightened girl cried aloud:

"Murder! Murder!"

And suddenly a captain of the king's guard came charging down the street on his horse to rescue the frightened gypsy. He snatched Esmeralda away from the startled Quasimodo. Quickly the wretch was surrounded by the captain's friends — others of the king's guard. They took hold of him and tied him up. He bellowed, he foamed at the mouth, he kicked, and he bit — but he couldn't get away. His master quietly slipped into the darkness and disappeared.

Esmeralda, meanwhile, stood up and looked into the captain's face. He was so handsome and strong, and a smile lit her face. "What is your name, sir?" she asked.

"Captain Phoebus, at your service, my dear," replied the captain.

"Thank you," she said. Then turning, she disappeared into the night.

But what of poor Quasimodo? The soldiers took him quickly to the Hall of Justice for punishment. Dumbly he stood. Since he couldn't hear the questions asked of him, he didn't answer. His silence enraged the judge.

"Guilty!" cried the judge. "Tomorrow morning let him be taken to the pillory at the Place de Grève. Let him be flogged and then turned for two hours. He shall pay for his rudeness!"

The Place de Grève was a favorite gathering place for the people of Paris. Here thieves and murderers were hung on the huge gallows. Here, also, poor wretches like Quasimodo were placed on the pillory and whipped. The citizens found the flogging and hangings great entertainment.

The pillory was a large flat wheel set up on a square stone. Here the next morning Quasimodo was placed on his hands and knees and tied securely with ropes. A burst of cheers and laughter went through the crowd when they recognized the ugly monster. They hooted when his shirt was removed and his hideous hunched back and hairy shoulders came into sight.

The Torturer was waiting to begin his duties. First, he set down an hour glass to time the flogging. Then he threw back his cloak. Over his left arm was a whip made up of

long strands of leather knotted with sharp bits of metal. He stamped his foot to give the signal, and slowly the wheel began to turn. The surprise on Quasimodo's face brought fresh shouts of laughter from the crowd.

All at once the Torturer raised his arm. The whip hissed through the air and came down on Quasimodo's back. For a moment, the poor monster used all his strength to try and escape from the cruel punishment, but escape was impossible even for a man of his tremendous strength. The muscles of his face twisted, and then he heaved a single sigh and turned his head to the side.

A second stroke of the whip followed the first. Then came another and another. The wheel continued to turn, and the blows fell. Blood began to trickle in a hundred little streams down the poor hunched back. Finally Quasimodo closed his only eye and did not move.

When the hour glass finally ran out, his punishment was not over yet. He still had to remain on the pillory another two hours. Only then would justice be satisfied. The wheel slowly continued to turn as the Torturer shook the blood off his whip. Quasimodo's poor, bleeding back and suffering face went round and round so that everyone might see. Now the good citizens of Paris began to shout and laugh and throw stones at the poor beaten wretch.

Quasimodo was deaf, but his one eye was very sharp. He saw the pleasure and mockery on the faces of the people. His face twisted in anger, and a growl came from deep in his throat. Hate, rage, and despair slowly spread over his hideous features. All at once the look of rage faded. A smile curved his twisted lips. A priest approached on a mule. It was none other than the Archdeacon Claude Frollo! But as soon as the priest saw his faithful dog Quasimodo, he dropped his eyes, dug his heels into the sides of the mule, and rode on.

Who could say what disappointment and despair entered the poor monster's heart as his only friend left him to suffer?

As more time passed, Quasimodo's mouth opened and like the roar of a wild beast came out one word: "Water!"

The crowd was delighted and laughed and jeered even harder.

"Water!" he cried again. He was answered with more shouts and laughter. A woman threw a stone at his head.

"That will teach you to frighten my children with your ugly face!" she called.

"Water!" roared Quasimodo for the third time.

Suddenly the crowd parted. It made way for a girl followed by a little white goat. Quasimodo recognized Esmeralda, the gypsy girl he had tried to carry off the night before. He thought that she was coming to take her revenge also. He watched as she gracefully climbed up on the huge stone.

Without uttering a word she took a flask from her belt and held it to Quasimodo's lips. Gently she poured a trickle of water down his parched throat. A second time she lifted the flask to his lips, and he drank greedily. Suddenly a big tear was seen to start from his dry and bloodshot eye. It was the first time he had cried since he arrived at manhood.

II

CAPTAIN PHOEBUS

Several weeks passed. The days were the same to Quasimodo. He continued to ring his bells and scurry and climb over the walkways and towers of his beloved Notre Dame. If he thought often of the young gypsy girl, no one was to know it.

Esmeralda, too, had many thoughts in her head. None of them, however, were of the ugly hunchback. Her thoughts instead were of a certain young, handsome captain of the king's guard — Phoebus. The name became magic for her. She looked for him everywhere as she danced in the streets.

Great crowds gathered to see her dainty feet move with quick, light steps as she beat on her tambourine. Her skirts whirled around her slim legs, and her lovely hair floated around her beautiful face. Many times she was rewarded by the sight of Phoebus on the edge of the crowd, and her heart beat wildly.

At last one day he spoke to her. "Will you meet me tonight, my lovely?" he asked softly. "We will go someplace quiet."

Her heart filled with joy, for she had come to love the handsome captain. Readily she agreed.

But while she had been watching the captain, someone else had been watching her. And on this day, the stranger overheard their conversation. He was draped in black and his face was covered by a hood. Under that black robe was none other than Dom Claude Frollo.

That night he followed the young couple to a room in a quiet house. When they weren't looking, he slipped behind them in the dark shadows and hid himself in a closet. His heart burned with jealousy as he watched Esmeralda lift her lovely face to the captain's.

"Do you hate me, Phoebus, for coming with you here alone? I think it is wrong of me."

"Hate you? Never, my lovely girl!"

At these words, Esmeralda's heart filled with delight and tenderness. She was silent for a moment, and then: "Oh, I love you, sir!" she cried. "You are so kind and handsome. You saved me that night from the horrible beast. I have dreamed of seeing you again."

Shyly she hung her head, and Phoebus took this opportunity to press a kiss on her white neck. The priest looking on gnashed his teeth in anger.

"Oh, Phoebus! Do you love me?" Esmeralda sighed. "I want you to tell me if you love me!"

"Do I love you, angel of my life?" exclaimed the captain. "I love you and only you!" The captain had said these words so often to so many women that they came very easily to his lips.

"Oh, I am so happy!" she cried.

Phoebus thought this was a good time to steal another kiss. That kiss brought new agony to the priest hiding in the closet.

"Oh, I love you! I adore you!" the captain said. "See if I don't make you the happiest girl in the world!"

"Yes, please, yes!" the girl sighed. "When can we be married?"

"Married!" the captain exclaimed in surprise — but his eyes filled with passion. "Pooh! Why should we want to be married? We can still stay together and enjoy each other." And his eyes began to glitter as they looked down at her lovely face and graceful figure.

Dom Claude, meanwhile, was in agony. The sight of the beautiful girl in the handsome captain's arms enraged him. All at once above the head of the captain Esmeralda saw another head — an angry, twisted face. Close to that face was a hand holding a dagger. The girl was struck speechless at the terrible sight. She saw the dagger plunge into the captain's back and rise again covered with blood.

Phoebus cried out — and fell. Esmeralda fainted. At the moment her eyes closed, she thought she felt a kiss burning like a hot iron on her lips.

When she awoke, she was surrounded by soldiers. The captain was carried away, covered with blood. The priest was gone. The window at the end of the room stood wide open. Just before she fainted again, she heard one man say to another:

"The gypsy witch has stabbed the captain!"

III

THE TRIAL

A great crowd filled the Hall of Justice. Almost as much as the people loved a good hanging and a good flogging, they loved a good trial.

Before the judges of the court stood Esmeralda. She was pale. Her hair — once so beautiful and neat — now hung in limp strings around her face. Her lips were white; her eyes were hollow. Alas! What a change the weeks in prison had brought.

"Girl," said the chief judge, "you are a gypsy. You are a witch cursed with the powers of Satan. You here stand accused of murdering one Captain Phoebus on the night of March 29. Do you deny the charge?"

"Yes, I deny it!" cried Esmeralda. "It was a priest — a devil of a priest who stabbed my Phoebus!"

"You were found alone in the room with the captain!" the judge roared. "Do you still deny it?"

"Yes, yes! Oh, sir, have pity on me! I am only a poor girl —"

"Take her away!" declared the judge. "Let her be tortured until she confesses her crime!"

In the cellars below the Hall of Justice was the torture chamber. In the middle of the room stood a wooden table. Leather straps were placed to hold the victim down. All around were the tools of torture — tongs glowing white hot in the fire, iron pincers with sharp pointed teeth like steel traps, vices to crush a hand or foot.

Poor Esmeralda took one look around her and grew

weak with horror. The Torturer stood over her. At his command, his two assistants strapped her to the table. Her foot was placed in a wooden vice.

"Do you confess your crimes?" asked the Torturer.

"I am innocent!" she cried.

"Then begin!" the man ordered. A screw in the vice was turned. Esmeralda gave one horrible cry of pain.

"Hold!" said the Torturer. "Now do you confess?"

"Yes, yes!" cried the miserable girl. "I confess everything! Anything! Only please let me go!"

That day Esmeralda was found guilty of murder and sentenced to hang in one week's time. Until then, she was thrown into the dungeon below the torture chamber. Anyone who had seen her dancing in the sunlight would have shuddered to see her now. Weighted down with chains she lay on the wet floor of her cell — cold as night, cold as death. No light entered the room. A little straw to sleep on, a pitcher of water, a crust of bread — these were all that she was allowed.

Her Phoebus was dead. She herself was to die on the gallows. What more could she suffer?

The night before she was to hang, the door to her cell opened. She saw a candle, a hand, a dark figure draped in black robes. "Who are you?" she cried.

"A priest," said the figure. "I have come to prepare you. You are to die tomorrow."

The light moved, and she looked into the priest's face. She gave a cry of pain. She knew that face! She had seen it before, and it had haunted her nightmares ever since. This was the man who had killed her beloved Phoebus!

"Who are you?" she cried again. "Why have you done this to me? Do you hate me so much?"

"Hate you?" Dom Claude said. "I love you!"

"Love? Never!" And the gypsy girl shuddered.

"Listen to me, Esmeralda! Before I saw you, I was happy. I was innocent. No one was as proud as I. Fasting, prayer, and study were all I needed in life. Then I saw you

dancing in the streets, and my life was changed in a flash. It was high noon. I saw you — a lovely creature with your flowing black hair and flashing eyes. Your arms, your feet, your whole body moved with such grace. I knew I had to have you! I watched you from the towers of Notre Dame. I waited for you in corners. Then I commanded my servant Quasimodo to capture you for me, but you escaped. Then that night a month ago, I followed you and your captain. I could not let him have you!"

"Oh, my Phoebus! My poor Phoebus!" was all she could say.

"No!" Dom Claude roared. "Do not call that name! You are mine! I love you! Say that you belong to me and only to me and I will save you from the gallows. You will be free. Promise to come with me, and we will escape!"

"Oh, my poor Phoebus! You murdered him! I would never go with you. Never! You are a devil!" With this final cry she fell face down on the floor. Only the splash of water dripping from the stone walls could be heard in the black cell.

IV

ON THE STEPS OF NOTRE DAME

Phoebus, meanwhile, was not dead. Men of that kind are hard to kill. When his men took him back to his rooms, he was bleeding and looked almost dead. No one bothered to find out if he lived or not. Justice didn't need the truth to find someone guilty. All justice demanded was a good hanging — and after all, the girl had confessed to killing him.

The captain was well in a few weeks, and Phoebus didn't worry much about what had happened to Esmeralda. He had another woman — a lady of beauty and fortune — and he planned to marry her.

The day of the hanging, Phoebus stood with his bride-to-be on the balcony of her home overlooking the front of Notre Dame. People were hurrying and scurrying below. Before the hanging the prisoner would be brought to the great church. She would stand outside the doors and repent of her sins.

Esmeralda was brought to the church in a cart. She had been stripped down to her petticoat. Her hair fell around her white shoulders. It would be cut before the rope was put around her neck.

"What in the world is the matter with you, Phoebus?" asked his lady. "You look quite shocked. Do you know that girl?"

"Me? No, no!" Phoebus cried. He was indeed shocked. The trial had taken place while he was still in bed recovering from his wounds, and he hadn't known that Esmeralda had been sentenced to die for his murder. And now did he care? No. Not enough to save her. He didn't care to have his name connected with a gypsy.

He forced a smile at his lady-love. "Me know a gypsy girl? Never!"

"Then let us stay and watch," the woman said, smiling.

The cart bearing Esmeralda stopped before the doors of the church. The crowd was silent as the soldiers led her to the steps. Chanting could be heard from inside, but the girl was too terrified to hear anything. Her eyes were fixed on the Archdeacon Claude Frollo who stood before her. He stooped as though to hear her confession.

"This is your last chance," he whispered. "Say you will be mine, and I will save you!"

"You are a monster!" she cried.

"Then die," said the priest. "No one will save you now."

She turned away from him and raised her eyes towards heaven. Then as her eyes dropped, she looked straight at the balcony where Phoebus stood with his lady. A scream of joy escaped from her lips. There was her love, her Phoebus — alive!

"Phoebus!" she cried. He hadn't heard her, she thought, as she saw him frown and lean down to the woman beside him. In a moment he had turned and gone into the house without a backward glance.

No one noticed the still figure over the doorway of the church. Except for his bright clothes — half red, half violet — he might have been taken for one of the gargoyles of the cathedral. At the beginning he had attached a knotted rope to one of the columns of the church. This done, he settled down to watch, unmoving.

Every eye was turned to Esmeralda. Suddenly, the still figure seized the rope with his hands and knees. He then slid down the face of the Cathedral like a drop of water down a window pane. In a flash, he grabbed Esmeralda, and quicker than lightning he was back up the rope, hold-

ing the girl under one arm like a doll. He shouted in a voice like thunder:

"Sanctuary!"

"Sanctuary! Sanctuary!" roared the crowd, and the clapping of ten thousand hands made Quasimodo's single eye sparkle with pride.

The shock brought Esmeralda's eyes open. She looked at Quasimodo and instantly closed them again, horror-stricken at the hideous sight of her rescuer.

Up, up Quasimodo climbed. Up the side of the church to the great tower. "Sanctuary! Sanctuary!" he cried as he carried his precious girl to safety. And below the crowds echoed: "Sanctuary!"

Once back on the roof, the ugly bell-ringer moved Esmeralda gently and held her tightly in his arms. His one eye looked down into the face of his treasure. It was full of love and pity. At that moment, Quasimodo was beautiful.

Below, the crowd shouted and cheered. They had been treated to a sight better than a hanging. The hideous monster Quasimodo had rescued the beautiful gypsy girl! The girl was free, for anyone entering the great Church of Notre Dame asking for protection — sanctuary — was safe. No one could touch her as long as she stayed within the church.

And was the priest, Claude Frollo, there to see the rescue of his love? No. When the girl refused him for the last time, he left the church to wander the streets of Paris, alone and miserable.

The thought of Esmeralda tortured him. He repented of nothing; he would do it all again. It was better to see her in the hands of the hangman than in the arms of the soldier. And yet he suffered so madly that there were moments when he tore his hair out in handfuls to see if it had not turned white.

A hurricane of despair was uprooting everything in his soul, but around him things were calm. Clouds sailed in a deep blue sky. A miller whistled as he watched the turning

sails of his mill. All this calm activity hurt him, and he turned to flee once more.

He wandered about the country. This fleeing from life, from himself, from God, went on all day. It grew dark, and his steps took him back to the church. He was almost afraid to look at it. Its front was dark, and the sky behind it glittered with stars. The crescent moon, in her flight upward, seemed to perch on the right-hand tower like a luminous bird.

It was midnight before he entered Notre Dame. "She is dead now," he said to himself. "Cold and dead." Inside the cathedral he paced the hallways. There was no peace or rest for him that night. Higher and higher he climbed in the church. Suddenly he saw before him a vision. A woman dressed in white appeared in the window of the tower across from him.

She was pale. Her hair fell over her shoulders as it had that morning. But there was no rope around her neck. Her hands were loose. She was free. But Dom Claude knew she was also dead. He was being haunted by her ghost! Then as suddenly as she appeared, she was gone. Dom Claude fell on his knees, too weak to stand. He was being haunted by the ghost of his beloved Esmeralda!

V

A HUMAN HEART
IN A FORM BARELY HUMAN

Each church had its place of sanctuary. In Notre Dame that place was a cell in one of the towers. It was here that Quasimodo took Esmeralda. It was here that Dom Claude saw his "ghost."

When Quasimodo carried her up the rope, the girl was half fainting with fear. The city was far below, and she had closed her eyes. From time to time she heard the loud laugh and harsh voice of the monster who held her. Then finally, she was laid down in a room. Huge, gentle hands loosened the cords that held her arms and hands. Two ideas only went through her mind: She was safe. Phoebus was alive.

Carefully she opened her eyes and looked at the ugly face above her. "Why did you save me?" she asked.

Quasimodo watched her anxiously, trying to guess what she had said. She repeated the question. Still he did not answer. Instead, he turned, and to her amazement he left her.

A few minutes later he returned, laid a bundle of clothes at her feet, and left once again. Quickly she dressed herself. The dress that he had brought her was the white robe of a nun. She had barely finished before Quasimodo returned. He brought a basket of food under one arm and a mattress under the other.

"Eat!" he said. "Sleep!" It was his own dinner and his own bed he had brought her.

31

Esmeralda lifted her eyes to his face to thank him, but she could not utter a word. The poor fellow was so hideous!

"Ah!" he said in his harsh, gruff voice. "I frighten you, I see. I am ugly enough. Do not look. Only listen. In the daytime you must stay here. At night you may walk all around the church. If you go outside they will catch you and kill you, and it will be the death of me, also, I think."

Once again she tried to thank him — but he was gone.

Next morning she opened her eyes to find him once more in the room. Quickly she closed them again, but in her mind she could still see his ugly face.

"Never mind," he sighed. "I am going. I only watch you while you sleep. That can't hurt you."

She made an effort to fight down her horror of him. "Wait!" she called, and when he didn't stop she laid a hand on his arm. Quasimodo trembled at her touch.

"Did you call me back?" he asked.

"Yes," she replied and nodded.

He understood the sign. "Ah, you must know I am deaf," he said sadly. "You thought that nothing could make me more terrible, but now you know. I must look like a beast to you. You are so beautiful. But you can talk to me with signs, if you wish, and I will watch your lips."

"Very well," she replied. "Tell me why you saved me."

"I understand," he said, nodding. "You have forgotten that you gave water to me when I was on the pillory. But I did not forget. Now I must go." He drew a whistle from his pocket and laid it on the floor. "I know I disgust you. I will stay away, but take this whistle. If you want me, blow it, and I will hear the sound."

Time passed on. Slowly Esmeralda began to recover from the terrible things that had happened to her. Always her thoughts turned to Phoebus. He was alive. That meant everything to her. Her love for him was as strong as ever. And surely he loved her too. He had told her so.

She still did not know what to make of her new friend

Quasimodo. She tried to like him, but she couldn't. He was too hideous. She never used the whistle, and he only came to bring her food.

One day as she leaned out of the window, she saw Phoebus riding by on his horse far below. "Phoebus! Phoebus!" she cried.

Quasimodo also saw the young and handsome captain. He sighed deeply. His heart was swollen with tears. He hit his fists against his head, and when he removed them, in each was a handful of red hair. Gnashing his teeth he cried:

"That is how a man should look. One needs only to be handsome on the *outside!*"

Still, Quasimodo hurried out of the church and after the captain. "Wait, captain!" he called. "There is someone who wants to see you — Esmeralda, the gypsy girl."

Before Quasimodo could move, Phoebus raised his whip and hit the poor wretch across the back. "The girl is nothing to me," he cried. "Be gone with you!" And he rode off.

The next morning when Esmeralda awoke, she found two vases of flowers beside her bed. One was a handsome crystal vase, but it was cracked. All the water had run out and the flowers were brown and wilted. The other vase was an ugly, rough pot of stoneware. The flowers in this, however, were fresh and sweet-smelling. Who can say why Esmeralda took the wilted flowers and held them to her breast?

Meanwhile, the Archdeacon Dom Claude learned the truth about Esmeralda's rescue. The woman he loved was alive and in his own church!

For many weeks he tried to forget her in study and prayer — but he could not. He could think of nothing but the girl and his faithful dog Quasimodo together. His soul raged with jealousy. For him to be jealous of the handsome captain was one thing, but to be jealous of a hideous beast was terrible!

Finally he could not stand it any longer. One night he took down the key to the staircase leading to the sanctuary cell and quietly crept up the winding steps to the tower.

Some sound made Esmeralda open her eyes. By the light of the moon she saw the face of the hated priest. Before she could move, Dom Claude had her in his arms.

"Be gone! Murderer!" she cried in rage and terror.

"Be kind to me, my love!" cried the priest. "My heart is on fire for you!"

"Let me go!" She hit out at him and dug her nails into his face. Still he did not loosen his hold. They were struggling on the floor, and suddenly her fingers touched the whistle. She raised it to her lips and blew.

Almost instantly the priest was taken in a painful grip. In the dark Quasimodo did not know that it was his master he held and pulled from the cell by one leg. But as he passed the window, the light of the moon fell on Dom Claude's face. With a cry, the bell-ringer let him go.

Shaking with rage, the priest kicked him viciously, ran down the stairs, and was gone.

VI

THE ATTACK ON NOTRE DAME

Esmeralda had been gone for many weeks now. She was gone, but her old friends had not forgotten her. And who were these old friends? They were the gypsies, of course, and the friends of the gypsies — every beggar and thief in Paris. All were outcasts of society, hated and feared by the citizens.

One day the news reached the King of the Gypsies that an order had come down from King Louis of France: Esmeralda, the gypsy girl, was to be taken from the Church of Notre Dame and put to death.

The gypsy king was determined to save her. He went to the King of Thieves and the King of Beggars. Together they would save the girl. They would break into Notre Dame, find the girl, and escape with her. Of course, on their way out, they would loot the church, taking with them the precious golden and bejeweled statues and crosses and other riches.

Meanwhile, Quasimodo kept watch over his beloved. He slept outside Esmeralda's door each night. Dom Claude treated him harshly, even striking him now and then. But Quasimodo continued to be the faithful servant — as long as the priest stayed away from the cell in the tower.

One day the bell-ringer noticed that several strange men were prowling around the church. He guessed that someone might be planning to harm the gypsy girl. Once night came, he stood watch on the balcony of the church. His one sharp eye searched the darkness for trouble.

Finally one night came when he saw an army of men slipping along the edge of the river and slinking along the streets and around corners. As they neared the church, a torch was lit, then another and another. In the light Quasimodo saw the terrible army of rabble — men and women dressed in rags. They were armed with axes, pitchforks, rocks, and clubs. The whole town was asleep. Only he saw the danger.

Outside the great front doors, the King of the Gypsies stood with his ragged soldiers. He raised his head and called: "Our sister's life is in danger. She has taken sanctuary in the church, but now the king has ordered her death. We have come to take her away!"

Quasimodo saw the king, of course, but he could not hear what he was saying. He only saw the king give an order and the rabble rush at the doors of the church. The doors were locked and barred, but how long would they hold?

"Come, men!" the gypsy king called. "Break down the doors!" But no sooner had he spoken than a great beam — a huge, rough log — came hurling down out of the sky, crushing a dozen men under it.

"It was an accident!" cried the king. "Get on with your work, men!" At the same instant he spoke, a shower of rocks dropped on the men below. Stones — some large boulders, some small — bashed in heads and broke arms and legs. A large heap of killed and wounded lay bleeding and dying under the rain of rocks.

Their enemy — although they didn't know it — was Quasimodo. As they first approached the church, he ran along the platform between the two towers. For several minutes he hadn't known what to do. Then he remembered that workmen had been busy the whole day repairing the walls and roof of the one tower. A room was filled with their tools and materials — beams, piles of stones and rolls of lead. Here he had found his weapons.

Now he looked down on the bloody army of thieves, beggars and gypsies. They were not giving up despite the

number who had been killed. Quickly he returned to the supply room. There he built a fire under a giant caldron filled with lead.

More and more fiercely the rabble worked at the doors below. They used the log as a battering ram to crash against the heavy, solid wood. The doors were nearly open. The wood was cracking. All of a sudden, a howl went up more terrible than any yet. Those who were not yelling looked around. A stream of hot, melted lead was pouring from the top of the building — right into the thickest part of the crowd. A sea of men fell beneath the boiling metal. The dying were roaring and screaming in agony. The sound was terrible. The new attack was too horrible to stand, and for the moment the rabble gave up and fled to safety.

All eyes raised to the top of Notre Dame. "Do you see that!" cried the gypsy king.

"Egad!" said the King of Thieves. " 'Tis that cursed bell-ringer — Quasimodo. Come, let us take him. Find ladders!"

Running quickly to the side of the building, they placed long ladders against the wall leading up to the balcony. As the first man reached the top, he didn't see Quasimodo crouching behind a statue, his eye flashing with fire. Out the beast came. He grabbed the man by one leg and one hand and swung him over the edge of the building. The thud at the bottom was like the sound of a coconut cracking. The broken body lay twisted and bleeding on the ground.

"Revenge! Revenge!" cried the rabble below. More ladders were set against the walls. As fast as he was able, Quasimodo pushed the ladders away with superhuman strength. Shrieks pierced the air as the ladders swayed and then fell, throwing the climbing men to their deaths. But he could not hold them off for long. He surely would have been killed if the cries from the great church had not sounded an alarm to the king's guards. As Quasimodo fought for his life and the safety of the gypsy girl in the tower, a whole column of troops arrived. At its head was Captain Phoebus. The king's guards attacked the rabble with swords and arrows. It was a fearful sight.

Meanwhile, windows were thrown open. The neighbors, hearing the shouts of the soldiers, took part in the attack. They threw a shower of rocks at the crowd below. At last the thieves were defeated. Those who were left alive ran in all directions, leaving the dead and wounded behind.

Now the fighting had ended, Quasimodo had one thought — to throw himself at the feet of his beloved Esmeralda. When he reached the cell, however, he found it empty.

And where was the Archdeacon Dom Claude through all the fighting? As the attack raged on, he rushed to Esmeralda's cell. Before she could resist, he threw his black cloak around her and dragged her out of the room, down the stairs, and through a small door in the back of the church.

"Help! Help!" she cried — but there was no one to hear her.

Her feeble strength was no match for the priest. He held her in a tight grip as he half dragged, half carried her over the rough pavement. At last they arrived at an open space. It was the Grève. In the middle stood the black cross of the gallows.

"Listen to me!" Dom Claude said harshly. She shuddered at the sound of his hated voice. "Your life is mine to give or take. Even now the king's guards are searching for you. Listen!"

In the distance Esmeralda could hear the crowds. "Where is the gypsy girl? Death! Death!"

"Esmeralda, I love you, but your time has come!" His bony finger pointed upward. "You see the gallows there? You must now choose between the gallows and me!"

"Let me go, monster!" she cried. "I tell you I belong to

my Phoebus. It is Phoebus I love. He is young and handsome. You are old and ugly. I will never be yours!"

"Then die!" Dom Claude snarled, gnashing his teeth. And he threw her from him and disappeared into the darkness.

Esmeralda pressed herself against the wall as the soldiers arrived. Then she saw him. At the head of the troops rode Captain Phoebus. He was there — her love, her Phoebus!

"Phoebus, Phoebus!" she cried.

He rode swiftly on, but one of the soldiers had heard her.

"Here is the girl we are seeking!" he cried.

"Call the hangman!" shouted another.

A third pointed to the gallows. "Well," he laughed, "we won't have to take her far."

Only one man turned his head sadly away: "Poor dancing girl!"

Esmeralda stared wildly at the soldiers. "Phoebus," she murmured.

"Hangman!" said a soldier as the man approached. "Finish this work. The king has ordered it!" And he dragged the girl towards the great black gallows.

Two men came forward to hold the trembling gypsy while the hangman slipped the noose around her neck. Then he lifted her onto his shoulders where she hung limply, too weak to fight any longer. Up the ladder the hangman went, onto the large stone block where the gallows stood black against the early morning sky.

VII

QUASIMODO'S REVENGE

During all this time, Quasimodo had searched frantically through the great cathedral. Finally, he was sure that Esmeralda was nowhere to be found. She had been stolen away from him.

Half out of his mind, he returned to the little cell. Empty! Still empty! With a cry he dashed his head against the wall and fell across the mattress on the floor. Wildly he rolled on the bed and kissed the place where his love had lain. Then he rose — bathed in sweat, panting, crying. Again he bashed his head against the wall — again and again and again. A second time he fell to the floor. At last he crawled out of the cell. He did not say a word. Every now and then a sob shook his great, hideous frame.

Who could have done it? Who could have taken her? For a long time he stared into space, thinking. Finally he had his answer. Only one person had a key to the staircase leading to the cell. Only one person could have taken Esmeralda away — Dom Claude, his master!

At that moment, dawn lit up the sky, and high above him on the balcony he saw the figure of a man. It was the Archdeacon. His heart was filled with rage. His past love for the priest warred with his love for the gypsy girl. Slowly he climbed the winding stair leading to the balcony above. Dom Claude stood with his back to the door. His eyes were fixed on the Place de Grève in the distance.

Quietly Quasimodo stole up behind him. He now saw what it was that captured the priest's attention. At the

Grève were gathered a few people and a great number of soldiers. The ladder was set up against the gallows. A man was carrying something white up the ladder. Quasimodo looked and then looked again. It was a young girl dressed in white. She had a rope around her neck. Quasimodo knew her! It was Esmeralda!

The man reached the top of the ladder. There he arranged the rope. Dom Claude was also watching intently. He leaned far out over the balcony to see better.

The hangman suddenly kicked the ladder away, and Quasimodo — who had not breathed for some moments — saw his love dangling at the end of the rope. Her feet were two or three yards above the stone slab. The rope made several turns, and Quasimodo saw the body of the girl twist and move in terrible convulsions.

From deep in the priest's throat came an evil laugh. It burst forth from his mouth. Quasimodo did not hear that laugh, but he saw it. The poor deformed monster watched Dom Claude in horror and took a step backwards. Then suddenly he rushed at his master and with his two huge hands picked him up and threw him over the railing.

The priest cried out as he fell. Wildly he reached out, caught at the gutter around the edge of the roof, and clung to it for his life. He was just opening his mouth to give a second cry when he saw the face of Quasimodo above his head. He was then silent. A two hundred foot drop was below him and Quasimodo was above him. Silently he twisted, trying to find a foothold, but his foot just slipped against the smooth stone.

At any time Quasimodo might have saved him by reaching out a hand, but the poor monster did not even look at him. He looked instead at the Grève. He looked at the gypsy girl. He looked at the gallows. He stood motionless and mute. Tears flowed in silence from his one eye.

The Archdeacon began to pant. Sweat trickled from his bald head, and blood oozed from the ends of his fingers. The gutter began to bend with his weight. While the priest

was going through the most terrible of agonies, Quasimodo kept his eye fixed on the gallows and wept.

Dom Claude's eyes began to start from his head. His hair stood on end. He began to lose his hold. His fingers slipped and his arms became weaker and weaker. His mouth foamed with rage and terror. Slowly his fingers relaxed their grasp — and down he fell.

Quasimodo watched as he slid over the tiles, off the roof to the pavement below. He did not stir again.

Quasimodo raised his eyes to the gypsy girl, dangling from the gallows. At that distance he could still see her quiver beneath her white robe in the last agonies of death. He then looked down at the Archdeacon stretched bloody and lifeless at the foot of the tower. A great sigh trembled in his twisted body.

"There is all I ever loved!" he cried.

On the day Esmeralda and Claude Frollo died, Quasimodo disappeared. He was never seen nor heard from again.

The night following the hanging of Esmeralda, her body was taken to a public vault. Here were thrown the bones and human remains from the dungeons and Paris gallows. Here rotted together both the guilty and the innocent.

About the mysterious disappearance of Quasimodo, all that we can discover is this: In the year 1484 people searching through the bones in the public vault came upon two skeletons — one male and one female. The bones were locked together. The remains of a white dress clung to the bones of the woman. The spine of the man was crooked and the head was sunken between the shoulders. The bones of the legs were twisted and deformed.

When those who found the skeletons tried to separate the bones of the man from the woman he held in a death grip, they crumbled into dust.

GLOSSARY

cathedral   (kə thē′ drəl)   an important church that is the official church of a bishop

deformed   (di formd′)   having a spoiled or ugly shape

flog   (flahg)   to hit with a rod or a whip

hideous   (hid′ ē əs)   very ugly or shocking to see

pillory   (pil′ ə rē)   a device for punishing people in public, made of a wooden frame with holes for the head and hands

rabble   (rab′ əl)   a disorganized crowd of people

repent   (ri pent′)   to feel sorry for bad things you have done

revenge   (ri venj′)   a way of hurting someone because you think that person has hurt you

sanctuary   (sang′ chə wer ē)   a holy place where people are protected